The McElderry Book of Mother Goose

also in the

**McElderry Books
Collection**

The McElderry Book of
Aesop's Fables

The McElderry Book of
Greek Myths

The McElderry Book of
Grimms' Fairy Tales

The McElderry Book of Mother Goose

Revered and Rare Rhymes
compiled and illustrated by

Petra Mathers

MARGARET K. McELDERRY BOOKS
New York London Toronto Sydney New Delhi

A Little Pig

A little pig found a **FIFTY-DOLLAR NOTE**,

And purchased a hat and a very fine coat,

With trousers, and stockings, and shoes,

Cravat, and shirt-collar, and gold-headed cane,

Then proud as could be, did march up the lane.

Said he, "I shall hear all the news."

B was cook **BETTY**,

A-baking a pie,

With ten or twelve apples

All piled up high.

C was a **CUSTARD**

In a glass dish,

With as much cinnamon

As you could wish.

A was an **ANGLER**,

Went out in a fog;

Who fished all the day,

And caught only a frog.

D was fat **DAN**,

Who did nothing but eat;

He would leave book and play

For a nice bit of meat.

E is an EGG
In a basket with more,
Which Peggy will sell
For a shilling a score.

G was a GREYHOUND,
As fleet as the wind;
In the race or the course
Left all others behind.

F is a FOX,
So cunning and sly,
Who looks at the hen-roost—
I need not say why.

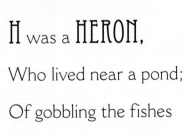

H was a HERON,
Who lived near a pond;
Of gobbling the fishes
He was wondrously fond.

3

I

I was the ICE

On which Billy would skate;

So up went his heels,

And down went his pate.

J

J was JOE JENKINS,

Who played on the fiddle.

He began twenty times,

But left off in the middle.

K

K was a KITTEN,

Who jumped at a cork,

And learned to eat mice

Without plate, knife, or fork.

L

L is a LARK,

Who sings us a song,

And wakes us betimes

Lest we sleep too long.

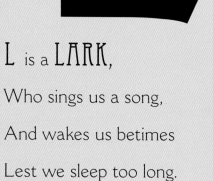

M

M was MISS MOLLY,

Who turned in her toes,

And hung down her head

Till her knees touched her nose.

N

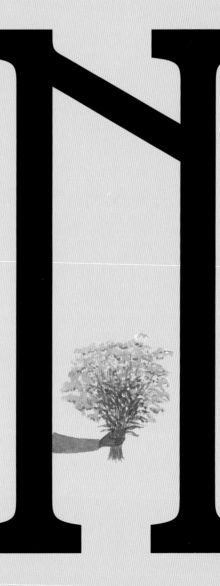

O

O is an OWL,

Who looks wondrously wise;

But he's watching a mouse

With his large round eyes.

N was a NOSEGAY,

Sprinkled with dew,

Pulled in the morning

And presented to you.

R is a RAVEN,

Perched on an oak,

Who with a gruff voice

Cries *croak, croak, croak!*

Q is the QUEEN,

Who governs the land,

And sits on a throne

Very lofty and grand.

P is a PARROT

With feathers like gold,

Who talks just as much

And no more than he's told.

6

S T U

S is a STORK

With a very long bill,

Who swallows down fishes

And frogs to his fill.

T is a TRUMPETER,

Blowing his horn,

Who tells us the news

As we rise in the morn.

U is a UNICORN,

Who, as it is said,

Wears an ivory bodkin

On his forehead.

V is a **VULTURE**,

Who eats a great deal,

Devouring a dog

Or a cat as a meal.

W was a **WATCHMAN**,

Who guarded the street,

Lest robbers or thieves

The good people should meet.

8

Y is the YEAR
That is passing away,
And still growing shorter
Every day.

X was King XERXES,
Who, if you don't know,
Reigned over Persia
A great while ago.

Z is a ZEBRA,
Whom you've heard of before;
So here ends my rhyme
Till I find you some more.

A Wise Old Owl

A wise old owl lived in an oak;

The more he saw, the less he spoke;

The less he spoke, the more he heard.

Why can't we all be like that wise old bird?

Anna Elise

Anna Elise,
she jumped with surprise;

The surprise was so quick,
it played her a trick;

The trick was so rare,
she jumped in a chair;

The chair was so frail,
she jumped in a pail;

The pail was so wet,
she jumped in a net;

The net was so small,
she jumped on a ball;

The ball was so round,
she jumped on the ground;

And ever since then she's been turning around.

As a Little Fat Man of Bombay

As a little fat man of Bombay

Was smoking one very hot day,

A bird called a snipe

Flew away with his pipe,

Which vexed the fat man of Bombay.

As Tommy Snooks
and Bessy Brooks

As Tommy Snooks and Bessy Brooks

Were walking out on Sunday,

Said Tommy Snooks to Bessy Brooks,

"Tomorrow will be Monday."

13

Betty Botter

Betty Botter bought some butter.

"But," she said, "the butter's bitter;

If I put it in my batter,

It will make my batter bitter.

But a bit of better butter

Will make my batter better."

So she bought a bit of butter

Better than her bitter butter,

And she put it in her batter,

And the batter was not bitter.

So 'twas better Betty Botter

Bought a bit of better butter.

Bye, O My Baby

Bye, O my baby.

When I was a lady,

My baby never did cry.

Now my baby is weeping

For want of good keeping—

Oh, I fear my poor baby will die!

Call John the Boatman

Call John the Boatman.

Call him again.

For loud roars the river

And fast falls the rain.

John is asleep.

He sleeps very sound.

His oars are at rest

And his boat lies aground.

Fast flows the river,

So rapid and deep,

That the louder you call John,

The sounder he'll sleep.

17

Doctor Foster

Doctor Foster went to GLOUCESTER

In a shower of rain;

He stepped in a puddle

Right up to his middle,

And never went there again.

From
WIBBLETON to WOBBLETON

From WIBBLETON to WOBBLETON

is fifteen miles.

From WOBBLETON to WIBBLETON

is fifteen miles.

From WIBBLETON to WOBBLETON,

From WOBBLETON to WIBBLETON,

From WIBBLETON to WOBBLETON

is fifteen miles.

Golden Slumbers

Golden slumbers kiss your eyes,

Smiles awake you when you rise;

Sleep, pretty baby, do not cry,

And I will sing a lullaby.

Gregory Griggs

Gregory Griggs, Gregory Griggs,

Had twenty-seven different wigs.

He wore them up, he wore them down,

To please the people of the town.

He wore them east, he wore them west,

But never could tell which he loved best.

Hector Protector

Hector Protector was dressed all in green;

Hector Protector was sent to the Queen.

The Queen did not like him,

Nor did the King;

So Hector Protector was sent back again.

Hey Diddle Diddle

Hey diddle diddle,

The cat and the fiddle,

The cow jumped over the moon;

The little dog laughed

To see such sport,

And the dish ran away with the spoon.

Hickory, Dickory, Dock

Hickory, dickory, dock,

The mouse ran up the clock.

The clock struck one.

The mouse ran down.

Hickory, dickory, dock.

24

Higglety, Pigglety, Pop!

Higglety, pigglety, pop!

The dog has eaten the mop.

The pig's in a hurry;

The cat's in a flurry.

Higglety, pigglety, pop!

Hinx, Minx, the Old Witch Winks

Hinx, minx, the old witch winks,

The fat begins to fry;

Nobody at home but Jumping Joan,

Father, Mother, and I.

Stick, stock, stone dead,

Blind man can't see;

Every knave will have a slave—

You or I must be he.

Hoddley, Poddley

Hoddley, poddley, puddle and fogs;

Cats are to marry the poodle dogs;

Cats in blue jackets and dogs in red hats,

What will become of the mice and rats?

How Many Miles to Babylon?

"How many miles to Babylon?"

"Three score miles and ten."

"Can I get there by candlelight?"

"Yes, and back again.

If your heels are nimble and light,

You may get there by candlelight."

I Do Not Like Thee, Doctor Fell

I do not like thee, Doctor Fell;

The reason why, I cannot tell;

But this I know, and know full well,

I do not like thee, Doctor Fell.

I Had a Little Husband

I had a little husband, no bigger than my thumb;

I put him in a pint pot and there I bid him drum.

I gave him some garters, to garter up his hose,

And a little pocket handkerchief to wipe his pretty nose.

I bought a little horse that galloped up and down;

I saddled him and bridled him, and sent him out of town.

I Need Not
Your Needles

The Baker's Answer to the Needle Peddler

I need not your needles, they're needless to me;

For kneading of needles were needless, you see;

But did my neat trousers but need to be kneed,

I then should have need of your needles indeed.

Jerry Hall

Jerry Hall:

He is so small,

A rat could eat him,

Hat and all.

Little Betty Pringle

Little Betty Pringle, she had a pig.

He was not very little and not very big.

When he was alive, he lived in clover,

But now he's dead and that's all over.

Johnny Pringle sat down and cried;

Betty Pringle, she lay down and died.

There was an end of one, two, three—

Johnny Pringle he,

Betty Pringle she,

And Piggy Wiggy.

Mary Had a Pretty Bird

Mary had a pretty bird,

   Feathers bright and yellow,

Slender legs—upon my word,

   He was a pretty fellow.

The sweetest notes he always sang,

   Which much delighted Mary;

And near the cage she'd ever sit,

   To hear her own canary.

Mother, May I Go and Swim?

"Mother, may I go and swim?"

"Yes, my darling daughter.

Fold your clothes up neat and trim,

And don't go near the water."

My Dame Has a Lame Crane

My dame has a lame crane.

My dame has a crane that is lame.

Pray, gentle Jane, let my dame's lame crane

Feed and come home again.

My Dear, Do You Know

My dear, do you know

How a long time ago,

Two poor little children,

Whose names I don't know,

Were stolen away on a fine summer's day

And left in the wood, as I've heard people say?

And when it was night,

So sad was their plight,

The sun it went down,

And the moon gave no light!

They sobbed and they sighed

And they bitterly cried;

And the poor little things,

They lay down and died.

And when they were dead,

The robins so red

Brought strawberry leaves

And over them spread.

And all the day long,

They sang them this song:

"Poor babes, poor babes, poor babes in the wood.

Oh, don't you remember the babes in the wood?"

My Mother Said

My mother said I never should

Go near the gypsies in the wood.

If I did, then she would say,

"Naughty girl to disobey.

"Your hair shan't curl and your shoes shan't shine.

You gypsy girl, you shan't be mine."

And my father said that if I did,

He'd rap my head with the teapot lid.

My mother said I never should

Go near the gypsies in the wood.

The wood was dark; the grass was green;

Out came Sal with his tambourine.

We went to the river, took a boat across,

Paid two shillings for an old blind horse.

Up on his back and off in a crack—

Tell my mother I shall never come back.

O Mother, I Shall Be Married

O Mother, I shall be married

To Mr. Punchinello,

To Mr. Punch,

To Mr. Joe,

To Mr. Nell,

To Mr. Lo,

Mr. Punchinello.

Oh, That I Were
Where I Would Be

Oh, that I were where I would be;

Then would I be where I am not.

But where I am, there I must be,

And where I would be, I cannot.

Punch and Judy

Punch and Judy

Fought for a pie;

Punch gave Judy

A knock in the eye.

Says Punch to Judy,

"Will you have any more?"

Says Judy to Punch,

"My eye is too sore."

46

Six Little Mice

Six little mice sat down to spin;

Pussy passed by and she peeped in.

"What are you doing, my little men?"

"Weaving coats for gentlemen."

"Shall I come in and cut your threads?"

"No, no, Mistress Pussy, you'd bite off our heads."

"Oh, no, I'll not; I'll help you to spin."

"That may be so, but you don't come in."

Ten Little Penguins

TEN little penguins went out to dine;

One choked his little self, and then there were nine.

NINE little penguins sat up very late;

One overslept himself, and then there were eight.

EIGHT little penguins traveling in Devon;

One said he'd stay there, and then there were seven.

SEVEN little penguins chopping up sticks;

One chopped himself in half, and then there were six.

SIX little penguins playing with a hive;

A bumblebee stung one, and then there were five.

FIVE little penguins going in for law;

One got in chancery, and then there were four.

FOUR little penguins going out to sea;

A red herring swallowed one, and then there were three.

THREE little penguins walking in the zoo;

A big bear hugged one, and then there were two.

TWO little penguins sitting in the sun;

One got frizzled up, and then there was one.

ONE little penguin living all alone;

He got married, and then there were none.

Terence McDiddler

Terence McDiddler,

The three-stringed fiddler,

Can charm, if you please,

The fish from the seas.

The Dogs of the Monks

The dogs of the monks

Of St. Bernard go

To help little children

Out of snow.

Each has a rum bottle

Under his chin,

Tied with a little bit

Of bobbin.

The Great Panjandrum*

She went into the garden

To cut a cabbage leaf

To make an apple pie.

And at the same time

A great she-bear, coming down the street,

Popped its head into the shop.

What! No soap?

So he died.

And she very imprudently married the barber.

And there were present

The Bobbelies, and the Joblillies,

And the Garyulies,

*A piece of nonsense written by the actor Samuel Foote (c 1754)
as a memory test for a fellow actor who claimed he could repeat anything
verbatim after hearing it only once.

And the great Panjandrum himself,

With the little round button at top.

And they all fell to playing the game of catch-as-catch-can,

Till the gunpowder ran out at the heels of their boots.

The Greedy Man

The greedy man is he who sits

And bites bits out of plates,

Or else takes up an almanac

And gobbles up the dates.

The Little Priest of Felton

The little priest of Felton,

He killed a mouse within his house,

And nobody there to help him.

The North Wind

The north wind doth blow,

And we shall have snow,

And what will the robin do then,

Poor thing?

He'll sit in the barn

And keep himself warm,

And hide his head under his wing,

Poor thing!

The north wind doth blow,

And we shall have snow,

And what shall the honeybee do then,

Poor thing?

In his hive he will stay,

Till the cold's passed away,

And then he'll come out in the spring,

Poor thing!

Rolled up like a ball

In his nest snug and small,

He'll sleep till warm weather comes back,

Poor thing!

The north wind doth blow,

And we shall have snow,

And what will the dormouse do then,

Poor thing?

The north wind doth blow,

 And we shall have snow,

And what will the children do then,

Poor things?

When lessons are done,

They'll jump, skip, and run,

And that's how they'll keep themselves warm,

Poor things!

59

The Queen of Hearts

The Queen of Hearts,

She made some tarts,

All on a summer's day.

The Knave of Hearts,

He stole the tarts,

And took them clean away.

The King of Hearts

Called for the tarts,

And beat the Knave full sore.

The Knave of Hearts

Brought back the tarts,

And vowed he'd steal no more.

There Once Was a Fish

There once was a fish.

(What more could you wish?)

He lived in the sea.

(Where else would he be?)

He was caught on a line.

(Whose line if not mine?)

So I brought him to you.

(What else should I do?)

61

There Was a Crooked Man

There was a crooked man,

And he walked a crooked mile.

He found a crooked sixpence

Against a crooked stile.

He bought a crooked cat,

Which caught a crooked mouse,

And they all lived together

In a little crooked house.

There Was a Little Woman

There was a little woman

As I've heard tell,

And she had three dozen

Eggs to sell.

She went to market,

All on market day,

And she fell asleep

On the king's highway.

By came a peddler;

His name was Stout.

He cut her petticoats

All round about.

He cut her petticoats

Up to her knees,

Which made the little woman

Shiver and sneeze.

"But if this is I,

As I do hope it be,

I have a little dog at home,

And he knows me;

And if it is I,

He'll wag his little tail,

And if it is not,

He'll loudly bark and wail."

When the little woman

Began to wake,

She was turning blue,

And began to shake.

She began to shake,

And she began to cry,

"Goodness mercy on me,

This cannot be I!

The poor little woman

Passed the night on a stile.

She shivered with cold;

Her teeth chattered the while.

She slept not a wink

But was all night awake,

And was mighty glad

When morning did break.

Home went the little woman,

All in the dark.

Up jumped the little dog

And began to bark.

He began to bark,

And she began to cry,

"Goodness mercy on me,

I see that I'm not I!"

She pinned on the piece,

And exclaimed, "What a catch!

What a bargain indeed—

It's a wonderful match!"

The dog wagged his tail,

And she started to cry,

"Goodness mercy on me,

I still am I!"

There came by the peddler

Returning from town.

She asked him for something

To match her short gown.

The sly peddler rogue

Showed the piece he'd purloined,

And said to the woman,

"It will look nice when it's joined."

There Was an Old Soldier from Bister

There was an old soldier from Bister,

Went walking one day with his sister,

When a cow at a poke

Tossed her into an oak

Before the old gentleman missed her.

There Was an Old Woman of Gloucester

There was an old woman of Gloucester,

Whose parrot two guineas it cost her.

But its tongue never ceasing

Was vastly displeasing

To the talkative woman of Gloucester.

There Was an Old Woman
Tossed Up in a Basket

There was an old woman tossed up in a basket,

Seventeen times as high as the moon;

Where she was going I couldn't but ask it,

For in her hand she carried a broom.

"Old woman, old woman, old woman," quoth I,

"Where are you going to up so high?"

"To brush the cobwebs out of the sky!"

"May I go with you?"

"Aye, by-and-by."

Three Wise Men

Three wise men of Gotham,

They went to sea in a bowl;

And if the bowl had been stronger,

My song had been longer.

Tweedledum and Tweedledee

Tweedledum and Tweedledee

Agreed to have a battle,

For Tweedledum said Tweedledee

Had spoiled his nice new rattle.

Just then flew by a monstrous crow,

As big as a tar barrel,

Which frightened both the heroes so,

They quite forgot their quarrel.

Twinkle, Twinkle, Little Star

Twinkle, twinkle, little star,

How I wonder what you are!

Up above the world so high,

Like a diamond in the sky.

Who Killed Cock Robin?

Who killed Cock Robin?

"I," said the Sparrow,

"With my bow and arrow,

I killed Cock Robin."

Who saw him die?

"I," said the Fly,

"With my little eye,

I saw him die."

Who caught his blood?

"I," said the Fish,*

"With my little dish,

I caught his blood."

"Fish" is short for "kingfisher."

Who'll make the shroud?

"I," said the Beetle,

"With my thread and needle,

I'll make the shroud."

Who'll dig his grave?

"I," said the Owl,

"With my pick and trowel,

I'll dig his grave."

Who'll be the parson?

"I," said the Rook,

"With my little book,

I'll be the parson."

Who'll be the clerk?

"I," said the Lark,

"If it's not after dark,

I'll be the clerk."

Who'll carry the link?

"I," said the Linnet,

"I'll fetch it in a minute,

I'll carry the link."

FARE WELL

Who'll be chief mourner?

"I," said the Dove,

"I mourn for my love,

I'll be chief mourner."

Who'll carry the coffin?

"I," said the Kite,

"If it's not through the night,

I'll carry the coffin."

Who'll bear the pall?

"We," said the Wren,

Both the cock and the hen,

"We'll bear the pall."

Who'll sing the psalm?

"I," said the Thrush,

As she sat on a bush,

"I'll sing the psalm."

Who'll toll the bell?

"I," said the Bull,*

"Because I can pull,

I'll toll the bell."

All the birds of the air

Fell a-sighing and a-sobbing,

When they heard the bell toll

For poor Cock Robin.

*"Bull" is short for "bullfinch."

Who Should Be Marching Up the Road

Who should be marching up the road,

But Little Pig in his very fine coat,

With his trousers, and stockings, and shoes,

Cravat, and shirt-collar, and gold-headed cane.

Proud as can be, he did come back again.

Said he, "I've just heard all the news."

Dear Reader,

When I did research for *The McElderry Book of Mother Goose*, I was amazed at how many rhymes had disappeared from recent collections. Perhaps lately Mother Goose books have been addressing only the very young, so the longer rhymes and the sad and scary ones have not been included. A big part of Mother Goose is based on real events, written down by people who were there when they happened hundreds of years ago. Naturally sad things happened alongside happy ones. I was pleased that I could pick a broad range of rhymes, some that are lesser known and some that are family favorites. To me this is "The Seldom Heard but Not Forgotten Mother Goose."

Petra Mathers

SOURCES

Baring-Gould, William S., and Ceil Baring-Gould. *The Annotated Mother Goose*. New York: C. N. Potter, 1962.
Opie, Iona, and Peter Opie, eds. *The Oxford Dictionary of Nursery Rhymes*. 2nd ed. New York: Oxford University Press, 1997.
————. *The Puffin Book of Nursery Rhymes*. New York: Penguin Group, 1997.
————. *Tail Feathers from Mother Goose: The Opie Rhyme Book*. Boston: Little Brown, 1988.
Vandergrift, Dr. Kay E. "Mother Goose: A Scholarly Exploration." New Jersey: Rutgers University Press. http://eclipse.rutgers.edu/goose

INDEX

MARGARET K. McELDERRY BOOKS

An imprint of Simon & Schuster Children's Publishing Division

1230 Avenue of the Americas, New York, New York 10020

Collection and illustrations copyright © 2012 by Petra Mathers

MARGARET K. McELDERRY BOOKS is a trademark of Simon & Schuster, Inc.

For information about special discounts for bulk purchases, please contact Simon & Schuster Special Sales

at 1-866-506-1949 or business@simonandschuster.com.

The Simon & Schuster Speakers Bureau can bring authors to your live event. For more information or to

book an event, contact the Simon & Schuster Speakers Bureau at 1-866-248-3049 or visit our website at

www.simonspeakers.com.

Book design by Debra Sfetsios-Conover

The text for this book is set in Canterbury Old Style.

The illustrations for this book are rendered in watercolor on Arches watercolor paper.

Manufactured in China

0612 SCP

2 4 6 8 10 9 7 5 3 1

Library of Congress Cataloging-in-Publication Data

Mother Goose. Selections.

The McElderry book of Mother Goose / illustrated by Petra Mathers.—1st ed.

p. cm.

Summary: An illustrated collection of Mother Goose nursery rhymes, including well-known ones such as

"Hey Diddle Diddle" and "The Queen of Hearts" and less familiar ones such as "Mother, May I Go and Swim?"

and "Ten Little Penguins."

ISBN 978-0-689-85605-1 (hardcover)

ISBN 978-1-4424-5314-2 (eBook)

1. Nursery rhymes. 2. Children's poetry. [1. Nursery rhymes.] I. Mathers, Petra, ill. II. Title.

III. Title: Book of Mother Goose.

PZ8.3.M85 2012

398.8—dc22

2011003404